NORMAN BRIDWELL
Clifford®
Makes a Friend

Hello Reader! — Level 1

SCHOLASTIC INC.
Cartwheel BOOKS®
New York   Toronto   London   Auckland   Sydney

The boy sees the dog.

The dog sees the boy.

The boy runs.

The dog runs.

The boy jumps.

The dog jumps.

The boy and the dog
spin and spin and spin.

The boy makes a face.

The dog makes a face.

The boy laughs.

The dog licks the boy.
He likes boys who laugh.

The boy does a cartwheel.

So does the dog.

They are friends.

• Word List •

a	face	runs
and	friends	sees
are	he	so
boy	jumps	spin
boys	laughs	the
cartwheel	licks	they
does	likes	who
dog	makes	

Hello, Family Members,

Learning to read is one of the most important accomplishments of early childhood. **Hello Reader!** books are designed to help children become skilled readers who like to read. Beginning readers learn to read by remembering frequently used words like "the," "is," and "and"; by using phonics skills to decode new words; and by interpreting picture and text clues. These books provide both the stories children enjoy and the structure they need to read fluently and independently. Here are suggestions for helping your child *before*, *during*, and *after* reading:

Before
- Look at the cover and pictures and have your child predict what the story is about.
- Read the story to your child.
- Encourage your child to chime in with familiar words and phrases.
- Echo read with your child by reading a line first and having your child read it after you do.

During
- Have your child think about a word he or she does not recognize right away. Provide hints such as "Let's see if we know the sounds" and "Have we read other words like this one?"
- Encourage your child to use phonics skills to sound out new words.
- Provide the word for your child when more assistance is needed so that he or she does not struggle and the experience of reading with you is a positive one.
- Encourage your child to have fun by reading with a lot of expression . . . like an actor!

After
- Have your child keep lists of interesting and favorite words.
- Encourage your child to read the books over and over again. Have him or her read to brothers, sisters, grandparents, and even teddy bears. Repeated readings develop confidence in young readers.
- Talk about the stories. Ask and answer questions. Share ideas about the funniest and most interesting characters and events in the stories.

I do hope that you and your child enjoy this book.

—Francie Alexander
Reading Specialist,
Scholastic's Instructional Publishing Group

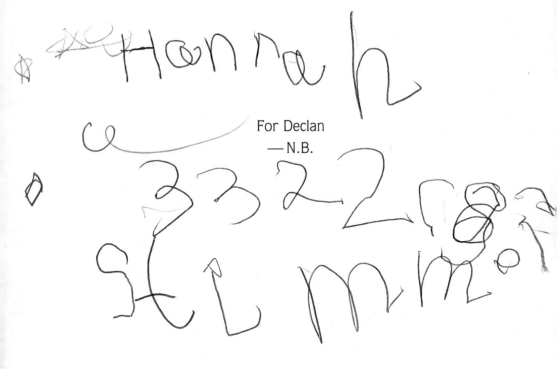

For Declan
—N.B.

Library of Congress Cataloging-in-Publication Data

Bridwell, Norman.
    Clifford makes a friend / by Norman Bridwell.
        p.   cm.— (Hello reader! Level 1)
    "Cartwheel Books."
    Summary: Because Clifford, the big red dog, imitates everything the boy does, he quickly makes a friend.
    ISBN 0-590-37930-5
    [1. Dogs — Fiction. 2. Imitation — Fiction. 3. Friendship — Fiction.]
I. Title II. Series.
PZ7.B7633Cjm   1998
[E] — dc21   98-14076
                                                                  CIP
                                                                   AC

13   14   15   16   17   18   19   20   01 02 03

Printed in the U.S.A.   24
First printing, July 1998